GREAT ILLUSTRATED CLASSICS

THE MAN IN THE IRON MASK

Alexander Dumas

adapted by
Raymond H. Harris

Illustrations by Brendan Lynch

BARONET BOOKS, New York, New York

GREAT ILLUSTRATED CLASSICS

edited by
Malvina G. Vogel

Published by Playmore Inc., Publishers,
230 Fifth Avenue, New York, N.Y. 10001
and Waldman Publishing Corp.,
570 Seventh Avenue, New York, N.Y. 10018

Printed in the United States of America

Contents

About the Author

The year was 1807. Five-year-old Alexander Dumas knew that he was different from the other boys in the small town of Villers-Cotterets, France. For Alexander was half-black and half-white. And nobody ever let him forget that.

Education bored young Alexander, and as he grew, he preferred spending his time hunting and leading an outdoor life. But when Alexander turned sixteen, his whole life changed. He saw his first play—a performance of Shakespeare's *Hamlet*, and from that moment on, his dream was to go to Paris and become a playwright.

Dumas worked for years as a clerk and wrote in his spare time. He had success writing plays and travel books. But it wasn't until 1844 that Alexander Dumas hit upon the one kind of story that was to make him rich and famous. That was the historical novel.

In his many historical novels, Dumas took people who really existed in French history and events that actually happened. He added main characters from his own imagination and created entertaining and amusing adventure stories around them.

Probably the most famous of these was *The Three Musketeers*, a tale of dashing young soldiers of the king who save the throne of France from shame. Dumas then took his daring musketeers—who now numbered four—on to further adventures in their career in *Twenty Years After*, then brought their lives and adventures to a close in the third book in the series, *The Man in the Iron Mask*—an adventure tale again involving the throne of France, this time with a mysterious impersonation that still has some historians puzzled to this day.

Alexander Dumas wrote more than six hundred books in his lifetime and made money from them, but died in 1870—penniless!

Recognizing an Old Friend

CHAPTER 1

A Visit to the Bastille

D'Artagnan, captain of the king's musketeers, sincerely regretted having to deliver his
friend Athos to prison.

As their carriages drew near the Bastille's
heavy gates, D'Artagnan pointed to a man just
getting out of a carriage up ahead. "Look yon-
der, Athos!" he cried. "I will wager anything it
is he."

"He? Who?" asked Athos, puzzled.

"It's Aramis, of all people!" D'Artagnan
replied.

Aramis, Athos, and D'Artagnan had been
friends since their days as guards in the king's

musketeers. D'Artagnan still recalled his adventures with Athos, Porthos, and Aramis — the Three Musketeers, they called themselves. The musketeers were soldiers who guarded the king of France. Only the bravest soldiers got to be musketeers. D'Artagnan had proven his bravery years ago when he helped the Three Musketeers save the queen of France from disgrace by recovering her stolen diamonds. After that, the Three Musketeers became the Four Musketeers, pledging, "One for all and all for one!" But that was twenty years ago, and the four friends had since gone their separate ways. Porthos had married a rich duchess, Athos had returned to his chateau, and Aramis had become a bishop of the Church. Only D'Artagnan had remained with the musketeers, and was now a captain.

"Aramis at the Bastille—arrested?" cried Athos. "Impossible!"

"I did not say he is arrested," said D'Artagnan. "He is alone in his carriage. Perhaps

"One for All and All for One!"

he is here to dine with Baisemeaux, the governor of the Bastille."

"Whatever for?" Athos wondered aloud.

"Let's see if we can find out," replied D'Artagnan. "Leave the talking to me; I have a plan." Then, as soon as Aramis had disappeared inside the building, D'Artagnan shouted to the guards, "To the governor!"

As the king's most trusted friend, D'Artagnan was accustomed to being obeyed. So, in a few minutes, he and Athos were shown into Baisemeaux's own dining room, where the governor and Aramis were about to sit down to supper. Both men looked up in surprise at the sight of D'Artagnan and Athos.

"Ah, there," said Aramis, "by what chance are—"

"Monsieur D'Artagnan! I... uh...." sputtered Baisemeaux, usually a pompous, talkative fellow who, for once, was at a loss for words.

"Governor! Have you forgotten our date?"

Baisemeaux's Unexpected Guests

cried D'Artagnan, pretending to look crestfallen.

Baisemeaux turned pale, then red, and finally stammered, "C-certainly not! I am delighted to see you. But—upon my honor— I have not the slightest—ah, but I have such a poor memory!"

"Well, perhaps I am wrong," said D'Artagnan, turning as if to leave.

"No, no! My dear captain, do sit down— you and your friend too," invited Baisemeaux. The last thing he wanted was to offend such a close friend of the king.

"Unfortunately, I cannot stay," said D'Artagnan. "I have important business at the palace."

Aramis and Baisemeaux looked at each other and breathed a sigh of relief. They had private business to discuss too—business that was not for the ears of the captain of the king's musketeers.

Meanwhile, D'Artagnan winked at Athos

"Do Sit Down."

and said, "Athos will join you, however, and I will return for dessert!"

Discomfort showed again on the faces of Aramis and Baisemeaux. It seemed they were not to dine in private, after all.

D'Artagnan took his "prisoner" aside and said softly, "Wait for me, Athos. Enjoy your supper. And don't let on that you're supposed to be dining in the dungeon instead of at the governor's table!"

D'Artagnan departed quickly and climbed into the carriage which had brought him, crying out to the coachman, "To the king! And burn the pavement!"

"To the King! And Burn the Pavement!"

D'Artagnan Reports to King Louis.

CHAPTER 2

D'Artagnan Pleads with the King

Arriving at the palace, D'Artagnan went directly to the king's chamber.

"Is it done?" inquired King Louis XIV.

"Yes, Sire," replied the captain of the musketeers in a grave voice. "Athos is now in the Bastille."

D'Artagnan's words made the king feel uneasy at having imprisoned Athos. Yet there was no choice. Athos' son had dared to love the same young woman the king loved, and Athos had defended his son, thus incurring the king's wrath.

"Did he attempt to escape?" asked the king.

"Not at all," said D'Artagnan. "I tried to give him a horse to make his getaway, but he wouldn't allow it."

"You betrayed me!" cried the king.

"Exactly so!"

Louis was unsure how to respond to such bold defiance. "I warn you—you are pushing your luck!" he said.

"On the contrary, Sire," said D'Artagnan politely. "I have come to get myself arrested too!"

"What? You?"

"Of course. My friend will be lonely in the Bastille. I propose that Your Majesty permit me to keep him company."

"Are you jesting, D'Artagnan?" cried the king, seizing a pen and paper. "Once I sign this arrest order, it is forever—a life sentence! Surely that is not what you wish."

"On the contrary, Sire," replied the musketeer. "Mine would have to be a life sentence, for once you imposed such a punish-

"Once I Sign This Arrest Order..."

ment on me, you would never be able to look me in the face again."

"Leave the room, Monsieur!" raged the king.

"Not until I've said what I came to say," replied D'Artagnan firmly. "Sire, you must choose! Do you wish to be surrounded by soldiers or slaves? By great men or puppets? Do you wish men to serve you or to crouch before you? If you prefer cowardice, then say it, Sire, and I will leave you. Then you may send me to the Bastille with my friend. That is all I have to say."

The king threw himself back in his chair, livid with rage. D'Artagnan's sincerity had pierced through his heart like a sword blade.

"Sire, here is my sword," continued D'Artagnan, drawing his sword from its scabbard and placing it on the table.

With a sweep of his hand, the king thrust it aside and it fell to the floor.

D'Artagnan's blood rose at this insult from

Thrusting D'Artagnan's Sword Aside

the king. "A king may exile a soldier," he declared. "He may even condemn him to death. But he has no right to cast dishonor on his sword! My sword shall not be returned to its sheath. Henceforth, it shall have no other sheath than my own heart!"

D'Artagnan snatched up his sword and, with a rapid movement, placed the hilt on the floor and directed its point towards his heart. "My blood be on your head!" he cried, starting to lean on the point.

The king threw his left arm around D'Artagnan's neck and, with his right hand, seized hold of the blade and returned it silently to its scabbard.

Then, badly shaken, the king returned to the table and picked up a pen. He wrote a few lines, then handed the paper to D'Artagnan.

"What is this paper, Sire?" asked the musketeer.

"An order for Monsieur D'Artagnan to set his friend at liberty immediately."

The King Seizes D'Artagnan's Sword.

D'Artagnan dropped to his knees and seized the king's hand and kissed it. Then, with neither the king nor the captain speaking another word, D'Artagnan left the chamber.

D'Artagnan had promised Baisemeaux to return in time for dessert, and he kept his word. Reaching the Bastille, D'Artagnan burst into the governor's dining room.

"Forgive my absence," he cried to Aramis and Baisemeaux. "But the truth is, my friends, that you, Aramis—a bishop of the Church, have been supping with a state criminal. And you, Baisemeaux, with your prisoner!"

The two men turned to stare at Athos, and Baisemeaux soon began to tremble at having dined with a man who had fallen into disfavor with the king.

"Here is the notice for his arrest and detention," continued D'Artagnan, handing an official document to Baisemeaux. "And here, my dear governor," he added, handing over a sec-

A Notice for Arrest!

ond paper, "is the order for his release! And now, I think that it would be best for Athos to return to his own chateau."

As Athos rose from the table, D'Artagnan turned to Aramis. "Perhaps you will ride back with us—"

"Thank you, my dear friend," said Aramis, "but I am afraid that is quite impossible. Affairs of state, you know."

D'Artagnan could well believe this. Aramis d'Herblay had fulfilled his lifelong ambition when he left the service of the musketeers—that of joining the Church. Now, as a bishop, Aramis played an important role in the Government of France. So, with keen glances that seemed to read Aramis' mind, D'Artagnan and Athos took their leave.

As the door closed behind the two old friends, Aramis turned to Baisemeaux, anxious to complete his business at the Bastille. "Now, Monsieur, you may conduct me to the prisoner."

"You May Conduct Me to the Prisoner."

Aramis Enters a Prison Cell.

CHAPTER 3

A Mysterious Prisoner

Deep in the Bastille, Aramis approached the form of a young man stretched upon his bed. A certain air of royalty seemed to cling to the prisoner, even in such dismal quarters. Aramis bowed and sat down.

"How does the Bastille agree with you?" began the bishop.

"Very well," replied the prisoner.

"You have need of nothing?"

"No."

"Not your liberty?" asked Aramis.

"What do you call liberty, Monsieur?" asked the youth. "I call liberty the flowers, the air,

29

light, the stars, the freedom to go wherever the nervous limbs of a 20-year-old man such as I may wish to carry me."

Aramis heard the bitterness in the prisoner's words…and understood the reason for it. Therefore, he could say nothing, only let the young man continue.

"Every prisoner has committed some crime for which he has been imprisoned," continued the youth. "But what crime have I committed? My conscience does not accuse me of anything."

"Hear me, my son," began Aramis softly. "Do you know who your parents are?"

"My childhood tutor used to tell me that my father and mother were dead."

"He was telling you the truth," explained Aramis, "but only partly. Your father is dead."

"And my mother?"

"She is dead for you," Aramis replied cryptically.

"Do You Know Who Your Parents Are?"

"Dead for me?" whispered the young man. "Then she lives for others, does she not?"

"Yes," said Aramis, his head bowed.

"And I, then," cried the young man, "what am I doing here, in the dark dungeons of the Bastille?"

Aramis looked long and hard at the prisoner sitting before him. "If you were to be free in the outside world, it would lead to the revelation of a great secret."

"My freedom reveal a secret?" asked the young man, bewildered.

Aramis hesitated for several moments. "Have you ever looked into a mirror?" he asked finally.

"Mirror? I have never been allowed to see a mirror," said the young man, "not even as a child."

"And there are none here, I see," remarked Aramis, looking around. "They have taken precautions. They have acted wisely."

"They? Who?"

"Have You Ever Looked into a Mirror?"

"Listen, my son, and I will tell you," began Aramis, "for the time has come for you to know the truth."

The young man leaned forward, eager not to miss any of the bishop's words.

"You know," commenced Aramis, "that the last reigning King of France was Louis XIII?"

"I do," answered the prisoner.

"Well, this king had long been worried that he would never have a son."

"And did Louis XIII die without one?"

"No," Aramis went on. "But for a long while he feared that he would be the last of his line. Then, unexpectedly, his wife, Anne of Austria, announced a happy event. And on the 5th of September, 1638, she gave birth to a son."

"But what has this to do with me?" asked the prisoner.

Aramis paused. "You are about to hear a story which only a few people could now tell, for it refers to a secret which is thought to be buried with the dead.

The Queen Gave Birth to a Son.

"Yes, on that September day, the queen gave birth to a son. But even while the court was rejoicing over the event and the king was sitting down to a celebration feast, the queen gave birth to a second son....Twins!

"The midwife ran at once to the banquet room and whispered to the king what had happened. He rose and left the table. But now the happiness that had earlier shone on his face was replaced with...terror! Terror—because the birth of twins threatened the line of succession to the throne. You see, the king feared that one twin might dispute the claim of the other to the throne, and so start a civil war in the kingdom."

A look of shocked realization spread over the prisoner's face. "Then, Monsieur," he gasped, "you mean that I... I am...?"

"Yes," confirmed Aramis, "you are the son of Louis XIII. You are Philippe, the twin brother of Louis XIV, and equal heir to the throne of France!"

Terror—Because of the Birth of Twins!

Aramis reached inside his robe and took out a miniature painting. "Here is a portrait of Louis XIV," he said, handing it to the prisoner.

The young man eagerly seized the portrait and gazed at it with devouring eyes.

"And now," continued Aramis, reaching inside his robe again, "here is a mirror."

The likeness was startling!

"I have brought all the documents, all the proof of your birth," Aramis assured the dazed young man. "Consult them, satisfy yourself that you are a king's son, and—" and here Aramis' voice rose forcefully, "and let us act!"

A Startling Likeness!

Porthos Welcomes D'Artagnan.

CHAPTER 4

Planning a Royal Party

The morning after his visit to the Bastille, D'Artagnan stopped by to visit his old friend, Porthos. He found the ex-musketeer standing beside his bed, half-dressed, and looking distressed as he surveyed a great number of fancy garments strewn all over the floor. But, at the sight of D'Artagnan in the doorway, Porthos' frown turned into a smile.

"Ah, D'Artagnan! Dear friend!" he cried. "You are always welcome, and just now more than ever."

"Well, Porthos!" exclaimed D'Artagnan, staring about the room. "Are you taking an inventory of your wardrobe? Here, I'll help you count them—"

"D'Artagnan, please!" pleaded Porthos. "This is no laughing matter."

"Is something wrong?" asked D'Artagnan, becoming serious.

"The fact is," said Porthos unhappily, "I have received an invitation to the king's party."

"Splendid!" cried D'Artagnan. "I shall be there too."

"Alas!" cried Porthos. "But I have nothing to wear!"

"Nothing to wear?" D'Artagnan inspected the room. "But I see more than fifty outfits on the floor."

"Fifty, yes," replied Porthos, "but not one that fits me."

"What? Haven't you always had your clothes made to order?"

"To be sure!" cried Porthos. "But my manservant, Mouston, has grown stouter.

Nothing Fits Porthos.

Much stouter than I am."

D'Artagnan was puzzled. "But what has Mouston got to do with the size of your clothes?" he asked.

"Mouston has always been kind enough to take my place at the tailor's," explained Porthos.

D'Artagnan tried to keep from laughing, but he could not. "Obviously, my dear Porthos," he said, chuckling, "there's nothing to do but order a new suit of clothes."

"But the party in honor of the king is only two days away," protested Porthos. "Who will make me anything by then?"

"The king's tailor, himself!" cried D'Artagnan. "Come along, Porthos. We have no time to lose."

D'Artagnan and Porthos hurried off to the shop of Monsieur Percerin, the most sought-after tailor in Paris. As they entered the work-room, the old man looked up with a smile of recognition and greeting.

Calling Upon the King's Tailor

"The captain of the musketeers will excuse me, I am sure," said Monsieur Percerin, "for I am very busy."

"Ah, yes," replied D'Artagnan, "on the king's clothes for the party, I presume. You are making three suits, they tell me."

"Five, my dear Monsieur," protested the tailor. "Five!"

"Indeed!" cried D'Artagnan. "And I am sure they will be beautiful. But I have brought you a customer, a very good friend of mine." And D'Artagnan indicated Porthos beside him.

"I will attend to Monsieur," said Percerin, "but not until later."

"Later?" cried Porthos. "When?"

"Why, when I have time," replied Percerin.

Suddenly, from behind a door leading into the fitting rooms, a new voice entered the conversation. "By no means later, Monsieur Percerin, if I ask you!" And then Aramis stepped into view.

"But I Have Brought You a Customer."

"Good morning, D'Artagnan! Good morning, Porthos!" exclaimed Aramis. "My dear friends! Monsieur Percerin will most certainly have time to make your outfit after all. Isn't that right?" added Aramis, turning to the tailor. It seemed that Aramis had an even greater influence over Percerin than D'Artagnan did.

"Monsieur," said Percerin to Porthos, "if you will follow me to the back, my assistants will take your measurements."

Delighted, Porthos left the room with the old man, while D'Artagnan remained with Aramis.

"Are you going to the king's party too, Aramis?" asked D'Artagnan.

"Yes," said Aramis with a smile, "but without a new suit."

"Well, then," said D'Artagnan, "so it is not a new suit that brings you to Monsieur Percerin?"

"No, no. I—that is...."

Aramis Changes Percerin's Mind.

"Ah!" exclaimed D'Artagnan. "You have some private business with Percerin? I shall go away."

"Some private business, yes," said Aramis, "but not private from you, D'Artagnan. Please stay and listen. We are, after all, old friends."

"Yes, indeed," replied D'Artagnan, most curious now about Aramis' business, and even somewhat suspicious.

Aramis turned then as the tailor returned to the room. "My dear Percerin," he began, "you are making five outfits for the king to wear, are you not?"

"Monsieur Le Bishop, you know everything!" marveled Percerin.

"And a great many more things too," murmured D'Artagnan.

"But what you do not know," cried the tailor in triumph, "what nobody knows, is the color and style of the king's new clothes."

"Well," said Aramis smoothly, "that is

Private Business—But Not from D'Artagnan

precisely what I have come to ask you!"

This request seemed so ridiculous to Percerin that first he laughed to himself, and then he laughed out loud. "Surely you jest!" he exclaimed.

"Not at all," replied Aramis. "At the party we wish to present the king with a portrait of himself. And that portrait ought to be dressed exactly as the king will be on the day it is presented." Then, turning to D'Artagnan for support, Aramis asked, "Is that not so?"

"Yes, my dear Aramis," agreed D'Artagnan, "and it is a brilliant idea." D'Artagnan was willing to go along with the story for the time being, though he didn't believe a word of it.

"Well, Monsieur Percerin," pressed Aramis, "what do you say to it?"

"I, uh—I don't...." Percerin hated to offend a good customer such as Aramis, but as a king's tailor, after all, he was sworn to secrecy.

"You are, of course, free to refuse," said

"Surely You Jest!"

Aramis. "I shall just have to say to the king, 'I had intended to present Your Majesty with your portrait, but Monsieur Percerin opposed the project.'"

"Opposed!" cried the tailor, terrified at being thought to oppose the king's pleasure. "Oh, 'tis not I who oppose it. Please, Monsieur D'Artagnan, you are my witness! Did I say no?"

D'Artagnan shrugged his shoulders neutrally.

"Come," said the tailor to the two men, "and you shall see both the patterns and fabric samples. I am sure the king will be surprised to no end by your present!"

And under his breath D'Artagnan muttered, "Personally, I don't doubt this for a minute!"

D'Artagnan Is Suspicious.

Aramis Returns to the Bastille.

CHAPTER 5

The Prisoner Makes His Escape

Aramis was most annoyed at having met D'Artagnan at the tailor's, for he knew that the musketeer did not entirely believe his story about the present for the king. "No," thought Aramis, "D'Artagnan will not be deceived for long. And once he is on to my scheme, neither friendship nor money will buy his silence. He is completely loyal to the king."

Aramis, therefore, was not in a very good mood when he arrived at the Bastille for the second time in as many days, but this time he had replaced his bishop's robes with the suit, boots, and sword of a cavalier.

Seven o'clock sounded from the great clock of the Bastille. "Seven o'clock—the supper hour of the unfortunate prisoners," thought Aramis as he sat down to dine with Baisemeaux. But his inner thoughts were masked by the unusually cordial smile he gave to the governor.

"Monseigneur," began Baisemeaux, calling Aramis by his official Church title.

"No, no," interrupted Aramis. "Call me 'Monsieur,' please," he said warmly. "I am not in bishop's dress this evening."

"Monsieur, then. I am honored to have you at my table," said Baisemeaux as he lifted a glass of wine in toast.

"Baisemeaux," replied Aramis, "let us get tipsy together tonight!"

"Bravo!" applauded Baisemeaux. "There is nothing I would like better!" Which was true, for Baisemeaux basked in the company of his superiors like a dog in the sun.

As he brought in their fifth bottle of wine, a

Toasting Each Other

servant delivered a message. "Monsieur Baisemeaux, an official order has arrived."

Aramis cocked his ear and listened. Yes, the plan he had arranged was now being put into operation.

"Leave it in the office," snapped Baisemeaux. "Can't you see we're busy?"

"Yes, Monsieur, b-but—" stammered the servant.

"Perhaps, my dear friend," began Aramis as he grasped the shoulder of the drunken Baisemeaux, "perhaps it is important."

"Oh, you're probably right," grumbled the governor. "But when one is at supper with such an esteemed companion—"

Aramis bowed politely, then gestured to Baisemeaux to read the orders. "What is it?" prodded Aramis carefully.

"An order of release!"

"There, now!" said Aramis. "That is good news, indeed, and worth disturbing us for."

"At 8 o'clock in the evening?"

"Perhaps It Is Important."

"I'm sure the unfortunate prisoner will forgive you."

"No doubt. But the prisoner shall be set free tomorrow morning, at daybreak."

"Tomorrow?" Aramis froze in fear, but he managed to hide his anxiety at the delay.

"At dawn," confirmed Baisemeaux.

"Why not this evening?" asked Aramis, pretending to be puzzled. "The message says 'Urgent!'"

"Because this evening we are at supper," said Baisemeaux, "and our affairs are urgent too!"

"Dear Baisemeaux," said Aramis, his voice suddenly silvery and warm, "even though I wear boots and a sword tonight, at this moment I talk to you as a priest. Cut short this poor man's suffering. God will repay you in Paradise."

"Oh, all right," grumbled Baisemeaux, rising to go. "I don't understand it, though. For ten years, they tell you, 'Watch this man well.'

"I Don't Understand It."

And then all of a sudden they write, 'Set him at liberty!' and add 'Urgent!'" Baisemeaux shrugged his shoulders.

The next moment, however, he stopped in his tracks. "Monseigneur," said Baisemeaux, "this order has not been countersigned. There must be two signatures for the release of a prisoner—the king's and one other. I shall send to the palace for instructions. This could be a forgery!"

"You are absolutely right," agreed Aramis, thinking quickly to prevent a disruption of his plans. "But if a superior officer gives you orders, you will obey?"

"Most certainly, Monseigneur."

"Well, Monsieur Baisemeaux, I, too, am going to write an order, and one whose signature you cannot question." Aramis' tone was suddenly cold and firm.

Baisemeaux turned pale at this icy change in the bishop's manner.

Aramis took a pen and paper from a nearby

"This Could Be a Forgery!"

desk and wrote out a command for Baisemeaux to carry out the order in question, signing it *Ad majorem Dei gloriam*—"By the grace of God."

Baisemeaux did not move an inch. If the original order was indeed forged with the king's name, then he—Baisemeaux—would be responsible for releasing a state criminal. But were these God's orders as well?

Aramis sensed the jailer's inner turmoil, and knew he had to reassure him. "Come, come, my dear Baisemeaux," he said. "You are a simpleton! Don't worry so!"

Baisemeaux finally bowed and left the room.

Aramis paced nervously until the man returned, followed by the youthful prisoner whom Aramis had visited the day before.

"And now, Monsieur," Baisemeaux was saying to the young man, "now that you are free, where do you intend to go?"

The prisoner looked around, as if expecting someone to come up with an answer.

Baisemeaux Returns with the Prisoner.

Aramis stepped forward. "I am a man of the Church, and here to render the gentleman whatever service he may please to ask."

The prisoner smiled and placed his arm through that of Aramis.

"Adieu, Baisemeaux!" said Aramis, and he and the young man speedily left the governor's apartment.

A carriage was waiting outside for Aramis, as planned. "Go on," he said to the driver, and the carriage rattled over the pavement of the Bastille courtyard.

Aramis barely breathed during the minutes it took to open all the gates at the moats. The prisoner, buried in a corner of the carriage, made no more sign of life than his companion.

At length, a jolt more severe than the others announced to them that they had cleared the last moat. Behind them closed the last gate. No more walls either on the right or left. Heaven everywhere, liberty everywhere, life everywhere!

A Carriage Is Waiting.

Aramis Outlines His Plan.

CHAPTER 6

Aramis Conspires with the Royal Twin

Aramis briefly outlined his plan to the newly liberated prisoner seated opposite him in the carriage. "You are Prince Philippe," he said, "the son of King Louis XIII and brother to Louis XIV. As such, you are the natural and legal heir to the throne of France.

"I have raised you from the depths of the Bastille for a great purpose, and I will place you above all the powers of the earth."

Here the prince challenged him. "Suppose one day you decide to hurl down the man whom you have raised. What is to stop you from, once again, deposing a king?"

"The day you are crowned," promised Aramis, "you are crowned forever! God has given you the appearance, the age, and the voice of your brother. Tomorrow you will sit upon his throne."

"Must my brother's blood be shed to accomplish this?" asked Philippe.

"Not at all," replied Aramis. "He shall take your place in the Bastille."

"Still, there are other problems," countered Philippe.

"State them, Prince."

"My brother is married."

"I will arrange for the Church to consent to a divorce," answered Aramis.

"Surely the imprisoned king will speak out and protest this from the Bastille."

"Protest this to whom—the walls? No one would listen to a raving prisoner. Why should they? He will look just like you!"

"You have taken care of everything," said the prince, "except for one thing."

The Promise of a Throne!

"And that is?"

"Conscience!" cried Philippe. "All that is good in me cries out against this plot!"

"And do you suppose your brother's conscience protested when you were imprisoned?"

The prince was silent.

"Now," Aramis went on, "I have sent Your Highness detailed notes to acquaint you with the different people who make up your brother's court. Have you studied the notes?"

"I know them by heart," the prince assured him.

"We shall see," replied Aramis. "Let us begin with your family. Your mother?"

"Anne of Austria."

"Your second brother?"

"A fine, dark young man with a pale face."

"Very good. Do you know the king's two chief advisors?"

"His prime minister, Colbert—an ugly man with dark brows and hair covering his forehead, ugly, but shrewd and intelligent."

Philippe Has Studied the Notes.

"And the other?"

"Ah, yes," said Prince Philippe. "He to whom the crown of France owes so much that it owes everything—the captain of the king's musketeers, D'Artagnan!"

"Yes, and be on your guard with him," warned Aramis. "It is an awkward situation. If he discovers our plot before I have revealed it to him in my own way, you and I will certainly be arrested or even killed. D'Artagnan is a man of action."

"I will keep that in mind," replied Philippe. "And you, Aramis, what will you get out of all this?"

"You shall elevate me to Cardinal of the Church," said Aramis, "and also appoint me your prime minister. And then you will secure my election as Pope."

"Agreed!" said the prince. "And so, tomorrow my brother will...disappear?"

"Exactly," said Aramis. "We will remove him from his bed by means of a secret plank in

"Be on Your Guard with D'Artagnan!"

his bedroom wall."

"But how will all this be accomplished?" asked Philippe.

"I have been making plans for some time," explained Aramis, "ever since the king agreed to visit Monsieur Fouquet."

"And does Fouquet know of your plans?"

"No, but he shall, when the time is ready. In the meanwhile, he has followed my suggestions for changes at his chateau, and my own workmen have followed my plans specifically. Yes, Prince, your brother will retire to his bed a king...and awaken a captive. From that moment on, you will rule. But the most urgent thing for you to remember is to keep me near you!"

"I well believe it, Monsieur!"

Changes Were Made at Fouquet's Chateau.

Fouquet and Aramis Await the King.

CHAPTER 7

The King's Party

The festivities were to take place at the Chateau de Vaux, the estate of Monsieur Fouquet, a wealthy nobleman and Louis' minister of finance. The chateau rivaled the king's own palace in splendor. Adorned inside with paintings and outside with statues and fountains, the estate almost glittered in the sun. An army of servants hurried to and fro as the guests anxiously awaited the arrival of the king and his attendants.

"To think that the king will be here in an hour!" said Monsieur Fouquet anxiously. Then turning to Aramis, who was standing nearby, he added, "Believe it or not, Monsieur, the king does not like me much, nor do I care much for him. But ever since he consented to visit my home—"

"Yes?" encouraged Aramis, suddenly interested in Monsieur Fouquet's words.

"He has become more dear to me. Do not laugh. He is my king. And I feel that if he were really to wish it, I could love that young man! But, listen, I hear the trumpeters."

In a short while, the king, preceded by trumpeters, guards, and D'Artagnan's troop of personal musketeers, presented himself at the gates of the Chateau de Vaux.

From the moment that Fouquet kissed the king's hand in greeting and throughout the excellent dinner, Fouquet was the perfect host. He was overjoyed at the king's pleasure, especially when Louis XIV exclaimed to him, "It is impossible, Monsieur, to dine better anywhere!"

Later, though, the king became gloomy and

The Procession Arrives at Vaux.

moody, worrying to himself, "Have I shown too much pleasure over Fouquet's food? Is his chateau even more magnificent, better furnished, and staffed by more servants than my own royal palace?"

Finally, as the evening drew to a close, the king was conducted with the greatest ceremony to his sleeping quarters. His chamber was the largest and handsomest in the chateau. Under Aramis' helpful direction, Monsieur Fouquet had had it completely redecorated in anticipation of the king's visit. The chamber's vaulted ceiling was painted with different scenes of slumber. Along with flowers and birds, the artist had also painted wizards and phantoms out of man's darkest dreams.

No sooner had the king entered the room than a cold shiver seemed to pass through him.

Meanwhile, D'Artagnan had decided to visit Aramis, whose room was on the floor above,

A Cold Shiver Passes Through the King.

directly over the king's.

"Do you know what idea occurred to me this evening, Aramis?" began D'Artagnan.

"No, tell me," replied his old friend with a smile.

"Well, the thought occurred to me that the true king of France is not Louis XIV!"

"What!" gasped Aramis, his smile now gone.

"No," said D'Artagnan, noting the instant of fear which showed on Aramis' face. "It is Monsieur Fouquet, who has given this magnificent party and behaved so splendidly."

"W-why, y-yes, of course," sputtered Aramis.

"And you, of course, have helped him immensely," D'Artagnan went on. "But was it necessary to refurnish the entire house?"

"When Monsieur Fouquet learned of the king's visit," began Aramis, now calmer, "he said that if he were rich enough, he would offer the king a chateau that was new from top to

An Instant of Fear on Aramis' Face!

bottom, inside and out. And that as soon as the king had left, he would burn the whole building and its contents, so that it might never be used by anyone else."

"Incredible!" exclaimed D'Artagnan. "And would you burn the portrait too?"

"What portrait?" asked Aramis, puzzled.

"Why, the portrait of the king—that surprise of yours," D'Artagnan reminded him. "The one for which you obtained suit patterns and samples of material from the tailor the other day."

"Oh, that!" said Aramis with a sigh of relief. "A little gift, that was all, to welcome the king to Vaux."

D'Artagnan went up to his friend and, looking him full in the eyes, said, "Aramis, that may be the story for everybody else to believe, but for me—"

"Upon my word, D'Artagnan," cried Aramis, "whatever do you mean?"

"My instincts tell me that you have some

D'Artagnan Doubts Aramis' Story.

concealed project afoot!"

"What nonsense!"

"I would swear to it," said the captain of the musketeers. "Oh, Aramis, we are not enemies; we are brothers and have been for many years! Tell me what you wish to undertake and, upon my word, if I cannot help you, I will swear to remain neutral!"

"I am undertaking nothing," insisted Aramis.

"Aramis, a voice speaks within me, and it has never yet deceived me. It is the king you are conspiring against!"

"The king!" exclaimed Aramis.

"The king, I repeat," said D'Artagnan firmly.

"Believe these words, my friend," said Aramis. "If I think of touching, even with my little finger, the son of Anne of Austria, the true king of France; if I have not the firm intention of kneeling before his throne; if tomorrow, here at Vaux, will not be the most

"We Are Not Enemies; We Are Brothers."

glorious day my king has ever enjoyed—may a bolt of lightning strike me down as I stand here before you!"

As Aramis spoke these words, he was close to an alcove draped over with heavy curtains. D'Artagnan, staring intently at his friend, did not notice the alcove, could not suspect that those curtains concealed a figure. Since the sincerity of his friend's words reassured the musketeer, he took hold of both of Aramis' hands, shook them warmly, then turned to go.

"Are you leaving so soon?" asked Aramis.

"Yes, my duty summons me. I will be on watch outside the king's chamber tonight."

"Then I shall see you in the morning," said Aramis, and they wished each other goodnight.

A Figure Concealed Behind the Curtains

Louis' Bed Begins to Sway.

CHAPTER 8

The Switch

While the two friends were talking in the chamber above, King Louis XIV gently closed his eyes and fell into a deep sleep. Then, as in a dream, it seemed to him that the god of sleep, painted on the ceiling, looked at him with eyes quite human. A human face seemed to move among the crowd of figures overhead. And what was even stranger—this face bore so close a likeness to his own that Louis fancied he was looking in a mirror.

His bed began to sway—a gentle, easy movement like a ship lapped by waves. Then it seemed to him as if the paintings on the ceiling were becoming smaller and darker. The bed seemed to be sinking away from them. Doubtless, the king was dreaming.

The light remaining in the royal chamber faded away and was replaced by darkness and gloom. No paintings or velvet hangings were to be seen; nothing but walls of a dull gray color.

"I am under the spell of some terrible dream," thought the king. "I must wake up!"

But even as he thought this, the king realized that not only was he awake, but that he had his eyes open too. Louis looked around him. On either side of his bed stood armed men wearing masks. Addressing himself to the nearest figure, the king demanded, "What is this—a jest?"

"It is no jest," replied the figure.

"Tell me what you want," pleaded the king, "and you shall have it."

"Will you be good enough to follow us?" was the curt reply.

"What Is This—a Jest?"

Then, without waiting for an answer, the masked men rudely pulled the king out of bed and shoved him along a winding passageway with many staircases leading out of it. As he stumbled along, Louis heard the sound of falling water over his head. Finally, the passageway ended at an iron door, which opened out into the balmy night air.

"Just what do you intend to do with the king of France?" Louis asked nervously.

"Try to forget that title," advised one of his captors.

"But tell me, at least, where we are going," begged the king.

"Come!" was all he was told, as the men helped him into a waiting carriage.

The carriage set off at a quick trot, and, some hours later, rumbled into the circular drive of the Bastille.

"Go and wake the governor," said the coachman to a guard at the gate.

Monsieur Baisemeaux soon appeared at the

The Passageway Ends at an Iron Door.

door, clad in his nightgown.

"What is the matter now, and whom have you brought me at this hour? Why, Monsieur!" exclaimed Baisemeaux, recognizing Aramis, his mask now removed.

"Hush!" said Aramis. "Let us go into your office."

"What brings you here at this hour?" repeated the governor.

"A mistake, my dear governor. It appears that you were quite right the other night."

"About what?"

"About that order of release," explained Aramis smoothly. "You remember that I persuaded you to release that poor prisoner without first checking with the king?"

"I told you something was wrong!" wailed the jailer.

"Yes, my dear Baisemeaux, it was all a mistake. You released the wrong man!"

"Alas! What is to be done about it!"

"Don't worry. I have recaptured him and

"What Brings You Here at This Hour?"

brought him back. He is in my carriage now!"

"Monsieur, how can I ever repay you?"

"By not saying a word of this to anyone," said Aramis. "And let no one talk with the prisoner. He is out of his mind, and thinks he is the king. But enough now—go and conduct the poor devil back to his dungeon."

As if in a trance, Louis entered the cell of his twin brother without a word. At first, he fancied he was dead, and that death—like sleep—had its own terrible dreams. Then a strange sound attracted his attention. He looked around to see an enormous rat calmly nibbling on a piece of dry bread. And Louis knew that he was, indeed, alive.

"A prisoner!" he cried out. "I-I am a prisoner! It must be a plot of Fouquet's, since I was in his house!

"There is a governor in this place," the king continued, in a fury of passion. "I will speak to him. I will summon him."

The king called, but no voice replied. He

"I-I Am a Prisoner!"

seized his chair and hurled it against the massive door, but no one responded. He pounded on the door, over and over, but with no better success.

Accustomed all his life to being obeyed, Louis trembled in rage at being ignored. His blood began to boil within him. By degrees his anger increased, until his fury knew no bounds.

Like a tiger, he leaped from the table to the window and shook the iron bars. He broke a pane of glass, and shouted out the window until his voice grew hoarse. For fully an hour he ranted on, until his strength was gone.

By morning—his hair matted on his forehead and his clothes in tatters—he could not be recognized as a king, a gentleman, or even a human being. And by then, the king clearly understood how thick the walls of a prison are.

A Fury That Knows No Bounds!

Philippe Feels Like an Intruder.

CHAPTER 9

The Plot Is Revealed

After the royal bed had deposited the king in the secret depths of an underground passage in the Chateau de Vaux, it rose again to its chamber. Likewise, the domed ceiling slowly sank under Aramis' touch, stopping several feet above the head of Louis' twin as he stood beside his brother's bed.

As Philippe looked upon the empty bed, still warm from his brother's body, he felt like an intruder.

"Away with this weakness!" he said to himself. "I, and I alone, should have occupied this bed if I had been left in my place in the royal cradle. Philippe, son of France, take your place on that bed!" And with these words he threw himself down on the king's bed.

Towards morning, a shadow glided into the royal chamber. "All is done, Sire," announced Aramis.

"Did he resist?" asked the new king.

"Oh, terribly. Tears and pleas."

"But in the end?"

"It was a complete success," Aramis answered him.

Just then there was a knock at the door.

"Who's that?" asked Philippe nervously.

"Probably someone your brother had an appointment with this morning," said Aramis, going to the door. "Let me handle it.... Ah, Monsieur Fouquet! You have come to see the king."

"Yes," whispered Fouquet, "and just between the two of us, I'm afraid he is most upset with me. He seemed angered at my attentions to his favorite lady of the court,

"It Was a Complete Success."

Mademoiselle La Valliere. But it was just politeness on my part."

"Don't give it another thought," replied Aramis, stepping out into the hallway. "The king wishes me to inform you that he is more than ever your friend, and that your beautiful party has touched him to the heart."

"What? I thought I was going to be arrested!"

"Come to my quarters," said Aramis, "and I will explain everything to you."

"Why is the king suddenly so pleased with me?" asked Fouquet, once they were seated in Aramis' chamber. "Is there something I do not know?"

"Yes," replied Aramis, knowing he could benefit from Fouquet as an ally.

"A secret?" Fouquet prodded.

"Yes, a secret. Do you remember the birth of Louis XIV?"

"As if it were yesterday."

"Have you heard anything—anything that

About to Reveal a Secret

might have sounded strange—about his birth?"

"Nothing."

"That is where my secret begins. And I shall share it with you. The queen was delivered of not one, but two sons. Twins."

"And the second is dead?"

"No. Both children grew up—the one on the throne, whom you serve. The other was brought up in the country, and then thrown into the Bastille. This poor prince was the unhappiest of men until God rescued him."

"Oh? In what way?"

"You will see. Being exactly alike, both ought to have been kings. Is that not so?"

"Certainly," agreed Fouquet. "Twins are one person in two bodies."

"I am glad to hear you say that." And Aramis walked softly all around the room, satisfied himself that they were alone, and then returned to Fouquet.

"Now, what does God do in order to

Aramis Makes Sure They Are Alone.

substitute one king for another?" Aramis asked.

"God sends his agent, Death, to seize one king and thus makes room for another. But don't tell me you have killed the king!" cried Fouquet.

"Not at all," murmured Aramis. "We have simply substituted one rightful king for another. For you see, God has formed them so like each other that only He could tell them apart!"

"What?" cried Fouquet. "What do you mean?"

"Go to the king's chamber," suggested Aramis, "and see for yourself."

"B-but the king!" stammered Fouquet.

"What king?" asked Aramis, in his gentlest tone. "The one who hates you and was going to have you arrested, or the one who likes you?"

"The king—of yesterday!"

"The king of yesterday—the crueler, the

"What Do You Mean?"

less intelligent king—has gone to take his brother's place in the Bastille."

"Great God! You have dethroned a king!" exclaimed Fouquet. "And to think that such a crime was committed here at Vaux! Under my roof!" Fouquet's voice came out half-strangled.

"Crime?" protested Aramis. "But he was going to ruin you. Have you forgotten that?"

"He was my guest; he was my king!"

Aramis trembled with rage. "You are speaking too loudly! Take care!"

"I will call out so loudly that the whole world will hear me," declared Fouquet.

"Have you lost your mind?"

"Not for a minute. You have dishonored me. I do not thank you for saving me from ruin. But I will at least not ruin you. I am going to the Bastille to rescue the true king of France. While I am gone, you will have four hours—four hours in which to leave France before King Louis sends his soldiers after you."

"Great God! You Have Dethroned a King!"

"Four hours?" sneered Aramis scornfully, "Where do you expect me to go in four hours?"

"It is more than you need to board a ship and flee to Belle-Isle, which I give to you as a place of refuge. Come, let us both go at once— you to save your life, I to save my honor."

And they left the room, with Fouquet leading Aramis down a secret staircase which led to an inner courtyard.

Listening as Fouquet galloped off, Aramis paused to collect his thoughts. "God! Demon! Lost, I am lost! What can be done? Flee to Belle-Isle alone? No, I shall take Porthos with me. My old friend will not question or refuse me."

Aramis strode quickly down the hall to his friend's room. After knocking at the door several times and getting no answer, Aramis turned the knob. Pushing the door open, he saw Porthos sound asleep.

Hurrying toward the bed, he shook his

Aramis Pauses to Collect His Thoughts.

friend. "Come Porthos. You must get up and dress quickly. We are going on a mission!"

Porthos obeyed, rising from his bed and opening his eyes even before opening his mind.

"And where are you two going in such a hurry this morning?" came a voice from the open doorway. It was D'Artagnan, standing there and regarding them curiously.

"My old friend," said Aramis to the captain of the musketeers, "there is no time now for explanations. All will be revealed to you soon. Now, take your leave of two old musketeers."

And the three of them embraced.

"Adieu, adieu!" And Aramis and Porthos were off.

"If it were anyone else," thought D'Artagnan as he watched his friends ride off, "I should say that those two were making an escape!"

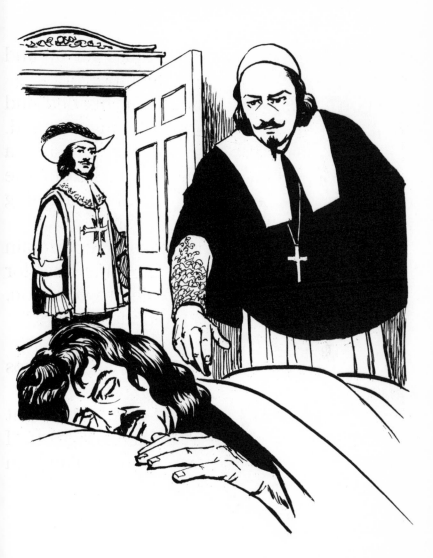

Aramis Wakes Porthos.

Into Baisemeaux's Quarters

CHAPTER 10

The King Is Rescued

Fouquet's carriage tore through the early morning mist. On the way, he trembled with horror at what had just been revealed to him. Arriving at the gates of the Bastille flushed and breathless, the nobleman stormed into Baisemeaux's quarters.

"Monsieur!" said Fouquet sharply.

Baisemeaux turned pale and wondered if he would ever grow accustomed to these unexpected visits from the king's friends.

"You have seen Monsieur Aramis this morning, have you not?" demanded Fouquet.

"Why, yes," answered the governor of the

Bastille. "He had some business to attend to here earlier."

"And are you not horrified at the crime which has been committed?"

"What crime are you talking about?"

"That for which you can be butchered alive, Monsieur! Do not forget that. Now, conduct me to the prisoner that Aramis brought here."

"Gladly, Monsieur," said Baisemeaux. "And if you have come here to remove him, so much the better."

"How do you mean?" asked Fouquet.

"Ever since his return, he has annoyed me extremely with his terrible fits of passion," explained the jailer.

"I will soon relieve you of his presence."

"Ah, so much the better!"

"Conduct me to his cell," ordered Fouquet.

"Certainly, if Monsieur will kindly give me the order."

"What order?"

Demanding the Prisoner Aramis Brought!

"An order from the king. I don't want to release the wrong man again."

"If you will allow me to see the prisoner," said Fouquet, "I will give you an order from the king at once."

"Give it to me now, Monsieur."

"If you refuse me, I will have you and all your officers arrested on the spot!"

"Stop!" cried Baisemeaux, throwing up his hands in despair. "I understand nothing of this whole affair, and I wash my hands of it. So, let us go."

Fouquet darted out of the room, followed by a moaning Baisemeaux.

"What a terrible morning!" wailed the jailer. "What a disgrace!"

"Walk faster!" cried Fouquet.

As they advanced up the spiral staircase certain smothered sounds became clear cries.

"What is that?" asked Fouquet.

"That is your prisoner!" said the governor "That is the way madmen howl."

"Walk Faster!"

Fouquet trembled. He had just heard, in one cry more terrible than all of the others, the voice of the king. "Give me the keys at once!" he cried, tearing them from the jailer's hand. "And leave this place!"

"I ask nothing better. This job will kill me, I am sure!" muttered Baisemeaux as he quickly withdrew.

The prisoner's cries became more and more terrible. "Help! Help! I am the king!"

Reaching the cell from which the cries were coming, Fouquet desperately tried one key after another.

The king, meanwhile, was shouting at the top of his voice. "It was Fouquet who brought me here! Help the king against Fouquet!"

Finally, one key fit, and the door flew open. Each man uttered a cry of horror upon seeing the other.

"Have you come to kill me, Monsieur?" cried the king as he recognized Fouquet.

"Oh, what a state for the king to be in,"

"Have You Come to Kill Me, Monsieur?"

murmured Fouquet, never having seen any
thing more terrible than the king's appearance
at that moment. Haggard, pale, foaming, his
clothes stained with sweat and blood, Louis XIV
was a picture of fear and despair.

"Sire," said Fouquet, "do you not recog
nize the most faithful of your subjects?"

"Faithful?" cried Louis. "You?"

Fouquet, his arms outstretched and his
eyes filled with tears, ran to Louis and knel
before him. "My king!" he cried. "How you
must have suffered!"

And Fouquet rapidly related to the king
the details of the incredible plot.

The king, speechless for a moment, could
only take hold of Fouquet's hand with such
warmth as to show his relief at his narrow
escape. Finally, Louis' voice returned. "You
have not seen this false king, then?" he asked.

"No, I have not," answered Fouquet. "But
I am told that he is a perfect double for You

"My King! How You Must Have Suffered!"

Majesty—your face, your hair, your build…."

"Whom have you seen, then?"

"The leader of the scheme—Monsieur Aramis d'Herblay!"

"Your friend?"

"He was my friend, Sire. But I have banished him from France. He is even now on his way to Belle-Isle, which I have given him as a place of refuge."

"My musketeers will capture Belle-Isle, and he shall be put to death! Let us return to Vaux and unmask the pretender—the man who is impersonating me."

As they left the prison, striding past a completely confused Baisemeaux, Fouquet gave the jailer an order authorizing the prisoner's release. It was signed: "Seen and approved, Louis XIV."

Baisemeaux tore out the few remaining hairs he had left on his head, and began to consider other lines of work.

A Completely Confused Jailer!

The False King Plays Out His Role.

CHAPTER 11

The Brothers Meet

In the royal chamber at Vaux, the false king was bravely playing out his role. He did not protest as servants came in to dress him that morning, for he had watched from above, the evening before, these rituals of dress. And now, he played the part of king like he was born to it.

As a result of Aramis' coaching, Philippe had little trouble recognizing his court and family. His looks, voice and manners were so like the king's that no one had the least suspicion. Philippe was beginning to feel quite at home in his new role.

Aramis' absence, however, had begun to alarm him, even though D'Artagnan was at his side throughout the morning. "Let Monsieur d'Herblay be informed that I wish to speak with him!" he ordered.

And various members of the court scurried off to seek the bishop.

His mother, Queen Anne, entered. Philippe took her hand and kissed it tenderly. Little did she know that in that kiss was a pardon for years of horrible suffering.

With her hand still in his, Philippe suddenly heard a voice that seemed to come out of nowhere.

"This way! This way! A few steps more, Sire!"

"It is Monsieur Fouquet," said D'Artagnan.

A terrible cry resounded from all corners of the chamber. Then, through the doorway of the secret stairs, Louis burst in, pale and wild-looking. Fouquet appeared behind him.

The queen-mother, still holding the hand

Louis Bursts In, Pale and Wild-Looking.

of one son, uttered a cry as she beheld the other. The two princes, both pale as death, measured each other with their eyes and appeared to be about to spring upon each other. The unheard–of likeness of face, shape, and height left the whole court speechless.

Fouquet was as surprised as anyone. "Aramis was right," he thought. "This newcomer is as pure a king as the other."

D'Artagnan realized at once that in this meeting of the two kings lay the answer to all the mystery of the past few days. "So this is what Aramis has been up to," he murmured.

Louis XIV turned and addressed himself to the queen. "My mother," he said, "do you not recognize your son?"

Queen Anne raised her arms towards heaven, unable to utter a single sound.

"My mother," said Philippe, from the other side of the room, "do you not recognize your son?"

And this time the queen, overcome with

"Do You Not Recognize Your Son?"

remorse at what she had done to her infant son years ago, sank back in a faint.

Suddenly, Louis XIV ran to one of the windows and tore open the shutters, letting the morning sun shine in. Then he bounded towards D'Artagnan and cried, "Look us in the face and say which is the real king!"

D'Artagnan saw that this brother was used to giving commands. And without hesitating, he walked straight up to Philippe and, laying his hand upon his shoulder, said, "Monsieur, you are my prisoner!"

Philippe did not stir from the spot where he seemed nailed to the floor. His eyes were fixed upon the king, his brother. In his silent stare, he was condemning him for all his past misfortunes...and for all the tortures to come.

Louis waved a pointed finger at the imposter and cried to D'Artagnan, "Conduct the prisoner to the island of Ste. Margaret. There, he shall be imprisoned and his face shall be covered with an iron mask...one which will

"Monsieur, You Are My Prisoner!"

remain on him forever!"

With that, Louis turned and stalked out of the room, forgetting his mother who sat motionless three steps away from the son she left a second time to be condemned to death.

Philippe turned to Queen Anne, and in a soft but agitated voice, whispered, "If I were not your son, I should curse you, my mother, for having made me so unhappy."

D'Artagnan felt a shudder go through his bones at this young man's cruel destiny. But the musketeer bowed respectfully to Philippe, saying, "Excuse me, Monsieur, but I must obey my king's orders."

"It is God's will," said Philippe quietly and with dignity. "I am ready."

Fouquet, impressed at the young man's noble acceptance of his fate, softly whispered to D'Artagnan, "Aramis was right. This one is quite as much a king as the other."

"More," replied D'Artagnan. "Much more."

A Son's Misery!

Imprisoned in an Iron Mask!

CHAPTER 12

The King's Revenge

With the false king safely imprisoned in an iron mask on the lonely island of Ste. Margaret, Louis XIV began his plans for an assault on Belle-Isle, where Porthos and Aramis had fled.

First, he summoned D'Artagnan. "Monsieur," commanded the king, "assemble the musketeers. You will go immediately and take possession of Belle-Isle. Your orders are to blow up the fortress and let no one escape. If you succeed in this mission, it will mean a promotion to marshal for you."

"What do you mean, *if* I succeed?" asked D'Artagnan. "I *shall* succeed!"

"But you have old friends on Belle-Isle," said the king. "It is not easy for a man like you to march over the bodies of his friends."

While assuring the king that his orders would be carried out, D'Artagnan nevertheless admitted to himself that the king was right. Except that he knew that men such as Aramis and Porthos were well able to take care of themselves... "especially with a little help from their old friend!" he decided. So, D'Artagnan gathered the royal forces and set sail for Belle-Isle without losing a moment.

Meanwhile, on the island fortress, just off the west coast of France, Aramis and Porthos anxiously scanned the horizon. The fishing boats, which had left the island two days ago, had failed to return to Belle-Isle.

"There is something strange in it, Porthos," murmured Aramis. "There has been no storm at sea. And even if every boat had perished, not a single plank has washed ashore."

"You are right," agreed Porthos. "And the

Aramis and Porthos Scan the Horizon.

last two boats on the island, which I sent in search of the others, have not returned either."

"What? You sent the last two boats—"

"In search of the others," finished Porthos simply.

"What have you done?" cried Aramis. "We are indeed lost! How shall we make our escape?"

"Escape?" exclaimed Porthos. "Why should we want to escape? You told me we were sent here by Monsieur Fouquet to collect taxes for the king. Kindly explain to me, if you will, just what we are doing here."

"I have deceived you, my worthy friend," began Aramis.

"In what way?"

"We are not serving the king—we are his prisoners! I have been banished for supporting a pretender to the throne. The plot failed, and I fled here, taking my good companion with me."

Confessing a Deception

"Then, we are rebels!" cried Porthos.

"Oh, dear Porthos, be calm! We shall get out of this."

"It is not that which upsets me. It is this ugly word, 'rebels'! My name is ruined forever."

"No, no, Porthos! You knew nothing of my plans; you have done nothing yourself. I alone am the author of the plot. I needed you, my old companion, and you came without asking questions. I will explain it all to the king."

"It is too late," said Porthos sadly, as he pointed out to sea. "Look on the horizon."

Aramis followed his friend's gaze to a white spot on the water. "A boat!"

"There are two!" cried Porthos, as another mast came into view. "Three! Four!"

"Five!" cried Aramis, in his turn. "Six! Seven! It is the royal fleet, Porthos. They have blockaded Belle-Isle! So that is what has happened to the fishing boats."

Aramis watched as the ships drew nearer.

"Look on the Horizon."

"The king will have his revenge, it seems. But we shall not go down without a fight!" he cried. "Let the cannoneers mount to their batteries, let the riflemen take their places!"

A small boat was lowered from the royal fleet's lead ship. The three rowers, bending to their oars, rowed toward the island and soon struck land at the foot of the fort. A uniformed officer jumped on shore and waved a letter in the air. Two soldiers escorted him to the pier, where Aramis and Porthos met them.

"From the captain of the king's musketeers!" said the officer smartly, and he handed over the letter with a flourish.

"From D'Artagnan!" exclaimed Porthos happily.

Aramis took the letter eagerly and read:

"Order of the king to take Belle-Isle; order to put the garrison to the sword if they resist; order to make prisoners all the men of the garrison.

(signed) D'Artagnan."

A Letter from D'Artagnan

Aramis turned pale and crushed the paper in his hands.

The officer continued. "Monsieur D'Artagnan told me to take you both on board my boat and bring you to him."

"Let us go at once!" cried Porthos, encouraged at the very thought of seeing their old friend.

But Aramis stopped him. "Are you mad?" he cried. "This could be a trap!" Then addressing the officer, Aramis went on, "You will return on board your vessel and tell the captain that we beg he will come himself to the island!"

"Yes, Monsieur," replied the officer, and returned to his waiting boat.

"If it is truly D'Artagnan," said Aramis, turning to his friend, "he will come to us."

"This Could Be a Trap!"

D'Artagnan Arrives.

CHAPTER 13

Orders from the King

"Hark!" cried Aramis on the pier a short while later. "A boat is landing, and some musketeers are getting out."

"It is D'Artagnan, no doubt," shouted Porthos in his thunderous voice.

"Yes, it is I," replied the captain of the musketeers, running lightly up the steps of the pier. "And glad to see you both safe. We must talk at once."

D'Artagnan then turned and addressed a young officer who was following him. "Monsieur, you may remain where you are. I will not require your protection for a few minutes."

"I'm sorry, Captain," replied the young man. "But I have orders not to allow you to talk privately with anyone on the island. I shall therefore be present at your interview!"

D'Artagnan trembled with rage. "Monsieur, you produced orders from the king to see the note which I sent here. I instantly showed it to you. Then you produced orders to come with me to the island. I did not hesitate; I brought you with me. But now you are alone with me, at the edge of a pier set in thirty feet of salt water. Think hard, Monsieur, before you cross me!"

"I am only following orders," maintained the officer firmly.

"Let me explain, Monsieur. I have been angry only six times in my life," said D'Artagnan softly, "and in the five times which have preceded this, I have killed my man."

The officer became pale under this threat, but stood fast. "Monsieur," he replied, "you are wrong in asking me to disobey my orders."

The Young Officer Refuses to Leave.

D'Artagnan raised his foot calmly to mount the rest of the steps, then turned round, sword in hand, to see if the officer would follow him.

The officer made a sign of the cross and followed.

"You are a brave man, Monsieur," said D'Artagnan. "But these gentlemen here are my friends."

"I know that, Monsieur," said the officer.

"Very well. Permit me, then, to speak to them without a witness."

"Monsieur D'Artagnan, if I allowed that, I would be breaking my word as a soldier. However, you are an honorable man. So go ahead, speak with your friends, and do not despise me for committing for you—and you alone—this dishonorable act of disobeying my orders."

"Thanks, a thousand thanks!" said D'Artagnan to the officer. "You have made yourself three friends for life." And he hastened to join Aramis and Porthos.

"You Are a Brave Man, Monsieur."

"Well," said D'Artagnan, reaching his friends and embracing them. "You can see the difficulty of my position. The king has ordered a blockade to intercept all vessels coming to or going from Belle-Isle. If you try to flee, your boat will be seized by the royal cruisers. If you remain here, their cannons will destroy the island. And that young officer over there has orders to prevent me from saving you. The king wants your heads, and he will have them!"

"We will remain at Belle-Isle," said Aramis "and I assure you, we will not surrender easily."

"Let us try something else first," said D'Artagnan. "I have an idea!" And he spoke rapidly and softly to Aramis alone.

Aramis listened intently, nodding as D'Artagnan spoke. At last, he cried, "Perfect!"

Moments later, D'Artagnan left Belle-Isle with his steadfast companion, the young officer.

Three Old Friends Embrace.

Returning on board his ship, D'Artagnan assembled his council, which consisted of all the officers serving under his command. "Gentlemen," he began, "I have been to Belle-Isle and found it to be a good and solid garrison. Moreover, preparations are being made for a defense which may prove troublesome. Therefore, I intend to send for two of the chief figures leading the defense. Once we separate them from their troops and cannons, we shall be better able to deal with them."

A major rose from his seat. "Monsieur," he said, "if the island is set upon rebellion, we should direct all our forces to the attack."

"I beg to differ," replied D'Artagnan. "Once the leaders come on board my vessel, I will impress them with the forces at our disposal. They will yield without fighting, and we shall have the island with very little effort on our part."

The officers around the table looked at one another, nodding. D'Artagnan's reasoning

D'Artagnan Assembles His Officers.

sounded good to all of them.

Abruptly, however, the young officer assigned by the king to follow D'Artagnan stood up and drew a folded paper from his pocket. He placed it in the hands of the captain.

"What! Another order?" exclaimed D'Artagnan in disgust.

"Read, Monsieur," said the officer.

D'Artagnan unfolded the paper and read these words:

"Monsieur D'Artagnan is hereby ordered not to assemble any council whatever, or to deliberate in any way before Belle-Isle has surrendered and the prisoners have been shot.

(Signed) Louis XIV."

The blow was direct; it was severe, deadly. But D'Artagnan did not give up yet. "Gentlemen," he said, turning to his officers again. "Since the king has charged someone other than myself with his secret orders, it must be because I no longer have his confidence. I will therefore go immediately and

"What! Another Order?"

carry my resignation to the king....To your posts, gentlemen. We are returning to France!"

D'Artagnan secretly triumphed while speaking these words. With the fleet en route for France and the blockade thus lifted, Aramis and Porthos might safely escape without fear of being captured.

"I suppose," D'Artagnan added bitingly, turning to the young officer, "you have no orders objecting to this?"

He did indeed. To this plan, the officer presented still another order from the king.

D'Artagnan read:

"From the moment that Monsieur D'Artagnan shall have expressed the desire to resign his post, he shall no longer be considered leader of the royal fleet, and every officer placed under his orders need no longer obey him.

(Signed) Louis XIV."

Brave and reckless as he was, D'Artagnan

Still Another Order from the King!

turned pale. A shudder ran through him. Every detail had been calculated against him.

"Monsieur," said the officer, coming up to him, "I shall be ready to depart as soon as you are."

"I am ready," replied D'Artagnan, subdued by forces he could no longer control.

The young officer immediately commanded a small boat from the fleet to convey the two of them back to France.

As they stepped into the skiff, D'Artagnan still hoped to reach the king in time, and plead for the lives of his friends.

Too late! The sound of a cannon rolled over the waters, then another, and two or three more still louder.

"They have opened fire upon Belle-Isle," said the young officer.

"They Have Opened Fire on Belle-Isle."

Revealing D'Artagnan's Plan to Porthos

CHAPTER 14

The Attack on Belle-Isle

After D'Artagnan had left Belle-Isle, Aramis and Porthos entered the fortress, where the bishop revealed to his friend what the captain of the musketeers had told him. "Porthos!" he said happily. "D'Artagnan has come through again. He has a plan!"

"Ah, indeed!" said Porthos. "Let me hear it."

"D'Artagnan is going to resign," explained Aramis. "He will command the fleet to return to France, and give his resignation to the king. While they're gone, we will get away. Or, rather, you will get away, Porthos, if there is

173

only a chance for one of us."

Porthos shook his head. "We will escape together, Aramis, or we will remain here together."

"You have a generous heart," said Aramis. "But why do you seem so distressed when freedom is so near?"

"I will tell you," said Porthos gravely, as he sat down at a desk. "I am making my will."

"Your will! Then you have given up all hope for escape?"

"I am tired," said Porthos. "It is the first time I have ever felt like this, and it has always meant death in my family."

"What on earth are you talking about?"

"My grandfather was twice as strong as I am," began Porthos.

"Then your grandfather must have been Samson himself," Aramis interrupted, smiling broadly.

"He was out hunting one day," continued Porthos, "when he felt his legs go weak. That

"I Am Making My Will."

had never happened to him before. He met a wild boar, and it attacked. My grandfather fired, but the shot missed. The beast ripped him apart."

"But why should that worry you now?" asked Aramis.

"Listen further," Porthos replied. "My father was as strong as a horse, and he never knew what it meant to be tired. One evening as he rose from the table, his legs failed him. He said to mother, 'Perhaps I shall meet a wild boar tonight, and join my father.' My mother laughed."

"Well?" said Aramis.

"Later that evening, my father decided to go down for a walk in the garden before going to bed. His foot slipped on the first stair, and he fell the length of the staircase. My father died on the spot."

"Two deaths don't make a third," Aramis reassured his friend. "Besides, when have your legs failed you? Why, you could carry a house

Two Deaths in Porthos' Family

on your shoulders right now!"

"Perhaps," said Porthos. "But lately I have been struck four times by this weakness."

Aramis pressed his friend's hand. "We will still live many years, my friend. By now, D'Artagnan must have issued his orders to clear the seas. And I have given instructions for a small boat to be brought to the cavern of Locmaria, here on the island."

"What good will that do us?" asked Porthos.

"Nobody knows about that grotto except for ourselves and a few hunters on the island. The king's men will be watching the harbor on the other side of the island. The grotto will be unguarded, and we shall escape from there."

"I understand," said Porthos, nodding.

"And your legs?"

"Oh, excellent—just now."

All at once, a cry sounded. "To arms! To arms!" repeated a hundred voices.

"It's the king's fleet!" cried one of Belle-

"We Will Still Live Many Years, My Friend."

Isle's own soldiers. "They're within half cannon shot."

"To arms!" cried Aramis, running to the pier.

"To arms!" echoed Porthos, following close behind.

And five minutes later, the cannonade began. These were the shots D'Artagnan heard. But the cannons on both sides did not have good aim, so the king's ships landed, and the fighting began hand to hand.

During one charge, Aramis turned to see Porthos stumble. "What's the matter, my friend?" he cried.

"Nothing, nothing—only my legs. They will be better when we charge again."

With that, Porthos and Aramis led their men in another charge that drove the king's soldiers back to their ships. This retreat, however, was only a trick. For on the other side of the island, another troop of the king's soldiers had landed. And the cannonade began

Porthos Stumbles During a Charge.

again, this time with better aim.

Learning of this, Aramis turned to Porthos. "We are lost, then," he said quietly.

Pale and downcast, he assembled the citizens of the island inside the fortress and spoke to them. "The soldiers of Louis XIV have taken the island," he began. "This time, it will no longer be fair combat—it will be a massacre. Surrender, in the name of the Lord."

Then Aramis turned to Porthos. "And now, my friend," he said, "let us try to make our own escape."

"But how?" asked Porthos.

"We shall escape by the cavern! Forward, my friend, our boat awaits us. The king has not caught us yet!"

Aramis Advises the Citizens to Surrender.

Reaching the Grotto of Locmaria

CHAPTER 15

In the Grotto

Midnight was advancing as Porthos and Aramis reached the grotto of Locmaria. Because it was black and forbidding, few men dared venture into the depths of its ancient caverns. Fewer still found their way out again. Those who had, including Aramis, knew that the cave consisted of a series of four chambers, each divided by enormous stone pillars.

The entrance to the third chamber was partly blocked by a vast boulder. Beyond, the roof of this chamber gradually descended, and the walls narrowed into a mere passageway. This rocky passage led to the fourth chamber,

185

which looked out onto the open sea.

As they were about to enter the first chamber, Aramis stopped Porthos. "Allow me, my friend, to pass in first. Three men inside are waiting for my signal."

"Go on, then," said Porthos. "Ah! There is that weakness—it has just struck me again."

Aramis left Porthos sitting at the entrance of the grotto. Signaling into the blackness with a cry like an owl, Aramis entered.

"Are you there, Yves?" he whispered.

"Yes, Monseigneur," came a whispered reply. "My two friends are with me—strong Bretons like myself."

"Good! Go to the entrance of the grotto and help my friend in," Aramis instructed them.

But Porthos, refreshed, needed no assistance, and entered on his own.

"Where is the boat?" Aramis asked Yves.

"Over there. But do not go too near with the light," warned Yves, "or you'll set off the gunpowder."

The Weakness Strikes Porthos Again.

"Very well," said Aramis, who began to examine the boat and its supplies closely nonetheless. The boat was long and light, equipped with oars and a sail. Aramis seemed pleased.

"Let us consider what to do," Aramis said to Porthos. "Shall we roll the boat down the beach and risk being seen? Or shall we continue on through the cave?"

"If you please," said Yves, "I know from my hunting days that the exit from the fourth chamber of the grotto is blocked by an enormous stone."

"I can lift it," said Porthos.

"Yes, I have heard that you have the strength of ten men," replied Yves. "But the grotto is dangerous."

"Yves is right," decided Aramis. "We'll leave by the beach."

As the robust Bretons were preparing to roll the boat out to the beach, the distant barking of dogs was heard. Aramis darted out of the

Aramis Examines the Boat.

grotto, followed by Porthos.

"It is a pack of hounds!" exclaimed Porthos. "They are upon a scent. Who can be hunting at a time like this?"

"Accursed dogs!" cried Aramis. "It is us they are hunting."

Within minutes, Aramis' fears were realized. The yelping pack of dogs closed in on the entrance to the cave. Aramis posted himself at a lookout between two rocks, and called back to his men, "It's the king's guards!"

At that moment, the hounds rushed into the grotto and filled the cavern with their deafening cries.

"Ah, the devil!" said Aramis, collecting his wits. "We have but one hope left. The dogs must not leave the cavern. Their masters must not come in after them and discover our boat."

Aramis turned to his companions. "The dogs will be forced to stop at the great stone. We will kill them there."

The Bretons sprang forward, knives in hand.

A Pack of Dogs Enters the Cave.

In a few minutes there was a concert of howls and then—nothing.

"Very good," said Aramis coolly, when the men reappeared. "Now for their masters!"

"What is to be done with them?" asked Porthos.

"Wait for their arrival, conceal ourselves and kill them," replied Aramis.

He took up a musket and placed his hunting knife between his teeth. The others armed themselves likewise.

The voices of soldiers could be heard outside the entrance. Then, a single guard entered and advanced blindly through the darkness. His way was immediately blocked by the barrel of Porthos' musket. The soldier raised his hand and laid hold of the icy weapon. At the same instant, Yves' knife fell upon the young man.

"Jacques! Jacques!" came voices from outside.

Aramis and Porthos listened as the soldiers cried out to their companion. "Into the grotto!

Yves' Knife Falls on the Soldier.

Into the grotto!" And the dim light of dawn revealed several human forms at the mouth of the cave.

"Fire!" commanded Aramis.

A discharge of musketry exploded in the cavern. At the same instant, cries and howls burst forth from the wounded. A second discharge resounded, and the few remaining forms drew back and reassembled outside.

"Is it the devil in there?" asked one of the terrified soldiers.

"Listen!" said another soldier. "Here come reinforcements!"

A company of guards, seventy-five strong, arrived at the Grotto of Locmaria.

"Where are the others?" cried the newly arrived soldiers.

"Dead!" And the survivors excitedly related their story.

"Into the grotto!" cried the troops, and they advanced into the blackness of the cavern together.

A Discharge of Musketry Explodes.

Porthos Lifts the Boat in His Great Arms.

CHAPTER 16

Seventy-Five Against Two

After the second discharge of musket fire had repulsed their attackers, Aramis quickly took stock of their situation. Clearly, they could not leave the grotto the way they had come. There was only one other way out. Beyond the great stone blocking the entrance to the third chamber, the tortuous passage led to the open sea. Aramis ordered the boat to be carried as far as the large boulder.

Porthos took the boat in his great arms and lifted it. He and the Bretons descended from the first chamber into the second, and arrived at the entrance to the third.

Setting down the boat, Porthos collected all his strength. Then, seizing the gigantic stone at its base, he applied his huge shoulders to it and gave one heave, then another, which made the wall crack. At the third shock, the stone gave way. Porthos braced his back against a nearby rock and shoved. The stone fell, and daylight rushed into the cavern from the outside. Then the three Bretons lifted the boat over the barricade.

From his lookout in the first chamber, Aramis watched the gathering soldiers. With the cavern about to be invaded, an escape by sea was no longer possible. The daylight, which now flooded the last two chambers, would expose their escape to the full view of the soldiers. And one discharge of their muskets would riddle the boat with holes, if it did not kill them all first.

Digging his hands into his hair with rage, Aramis called on both God and the devil for help.

Seizing the Gigantic Stone at Its Base

When Porthos returned, Aramis announced, "More soldiers are about to storm the grotto."

"How many are out there?" asked Porthos.

"More than seventy-five, now. We could kill about fifteen of them with our muskets, but no more."

"Ah!" said Porthos quickly. "What is to be done then?"

"We must think of something quickly, while the Bretons get our boat into the sea."

Porthos thought for a moment, then cried, "I've got it! I will place myself behind the pillar with this iron bar, then let it fall on their skulls as they come through!"

"Excellent, my dear friend, perfect! I approve your plan greatly! Except that you will only frighten them, and half of them will remain outside. What we want is the destruction of the entire troop. A single man left standing ruins us!"

"You are right," agreed Porthos. "But there are only two of us and seventy-five of them!"

Aramis and Porthos Plan Their Strategy.

"I have an idea," said Aramis. "Go ahead with your ambush."

"But what about you?"

"Don't worry about me; I have my own work. Quick, I hear voices. To your post!"

As Porthos stepped just inside the second chamber, holding in his hand a 50-pound iron bar, Aramis glided into the third.

Outside, a command was issued and twenty-five men charged into the first chamber of the grotto. But as they stepped through the narrow passage into the second cavern, Porthos' iron bar fell upon each soldier's head.

The advancing soldiers could see nothing. They stumbled over dead bodies, but still they came forward, walking in blood. The iron bar wiped out the first platoon without a single sound of warning to the second platoon, which was close behind.

But the second platoon had uprooted a thin fir tree growing on the shore. Twisting its branches together, their lieutenant had made a

Porthos Wipes Out the First Platoon.

torch, which now lit the cavern.

Peering over the lieutenant's shoulders, the soldiers drew back in terror at the sight before them. No firing had answered their own, and yet their way was stopped by a heap of dead bodies.

The lieutenant stepped backwards towards the pillar that concealed Porthos. Suddenly, a gigantic hand reached out and fastened on his throat. His outstretched arms beat the air as he uttered a stifled rattle. The torch fell and was snuffed out in blood. A second later, the corpse of the lieutenant added another body to the heap of dead that blocked up the passage.

The second platoon fired a volley of musketry, which flamed, thundered, and echoed in the cavern. The explosion caused enormous fragments of stone to rain down from the roof of the vault.

A deep silence followed, broken only by the footsteps of the third platoon, now entering the grotto.

A Gigantic Hand Reaches Out.

"Throw It Amidst Our Enemies."

CHAPTER 17

The Death of a Giant

Porthos felt a gentle touch on his arm. A voice murmured in his ear, "Come!"

"Oh!" said Porthos.

"Hush!" said Aramis, still more softly. And leading Porthos into the third chamber, he showed him a barrel of gunpowder weighing from 70 to 80 pounds. A fuse extended from one end.

"My friend," he said to Porthos, "take this barrel, light the fuse, and throw it amidst our enemies. Can you do so?"

"Light it!" replied Porthos, and he lifted the barrel with one hand.

"Wait until they are all massed together," instructed Aramis, "and then hurl it in their midst."

"Light it!" repeated Porthos.

"I will join the Bretons in the boat," continued Aramis, "and we'll wait for you on shore. Throw your barrel strongly, and then run!"

"Light it!" said Porthos a third time.

Aramis gave the burning match to Porthos and hurried out the fourth chamber and to the boat.

Porthos put the match to the fuse. For two seconds, the burning wick lit up the cavern. The terrified soldiers beheld a giant, surrounded by a heap of bleeding bodies. They saw the barrel of gunpowder in his hand, and understood at once what was going to happen. Together, they uttered one terrible shriek of agony.

Some tried to flee, but they fell over the bodies of other men. An officer of the third pla-

"Light It!"

toon ordered his men to fire upon Porthos. But their shots hit other soldiers, or bounced off the walls of the vault.

Porthos replied with a burst of laughter. Then, the arm of the giant swung round. Like a falling star, the barrel flew through the air and fell among the shrieking soldiers.

Porthos fled as Aramis had directed him, and reached the fourth chamber. Air, light, and sunshine greeted him. A hundred paces beyond, their boat danced upon the waves. There were his friends.

There was liberty. There was life after victory. Six more strides and he would be out of the cavern. Two or three vigorous springs more and he would reach the boat.

Suddenly, he felt his knees give way. His legs yielded under him. "Oh, no!" he cried. "There is my weakness again. I can walk no farther!"

Watching from the boat, Aramis called out to him. "Come on, Porthos! Come quickly!"

The Barrel Flies Through the Air.

"No! gasped the giant, making an effort with every muscle of his body. "No, I cannot!"

He fell upon his knees, but his great hands clung to the rocks of the cavern, and he raised himself up again.

"Quick! Quick!" urged Aramis, bending forward toward the shore, as if to draw Porthos to him with his arms.

"H-here I am," stammered Porthos, collecting all his strength to make one step more.

"In the name of Heaven, Porthos, make haste!" shouted Aramis. "The barrel will blow up!"

But there was no longer time. The terrible thunder of the explosion split the rocks of the cavern like wood under an axe. A jet of fire, smoke, and dust sprang up from the middle of the grotto. The sea flowed back as if driven by the blast of fire from the cavern. Cries, howls, and lives were all smothered in one great crash, as the first three chambers collapsed into each other.

"H-Here I Am."

This frightful shock seemed to restore strength to Porthos, and he rose to his feet. But at the same moment, the walls of the fourth chamber, no longer supported by the others, began to fall in. Porthos extended his vast hands to the right and left. A gigantic boulder came to rest on each. He bent his head, and a third granite mass sank between his shoulders.

For a moment, Porthos stood framed in granite. Then the rocks, which would have been enough to crush ten men, pressed him to his knees. The giant fell without uttering a cry for help. His arms stiffened for one last effort, then gave way. His shoulders sank.

Aramis sprang out of the boat. "Porthos! Porthos!" he cried. "Where are you? Speak!"

The last sighs of the valiant giant guided him amidst the ruins. In a surge of strength, Aramis put his shoulder to the mass of rocks.

The immense tomb gave slightly, and Aramis caught a glimpse of the still brilliant

Standing Framed in Granite!

eyes of his friend.

Leaving one man to guard the boat, two of the Bretons rushed up with their iron levers, and united their strength with Aramis'. But their efforts were in vain. The three men slowly gave up with cries of grief.

From his rocky tomb, Porthos watched them exhaust themselves in a hopeless struggle. "Too heavy!" protested the rough voice of Porthos in a final gasp.

Then the eyes darkened and closed. The giant head sank down, with Porthos breathing his last sigh. With him sank the rock, which even in his agony he had held up.

The three men dropped their levers. Then, breathless and pale, Aramis knelt down and listened at the stone for signs of life from his friend. Nothing more! Porthos slept the eternal sleep, in the tomb which God had made to fit his measure.

Their Efforts Are in Vain!

The Bretons Carry Aramis to the Boat.

CHAPTER 18

Aramis Surrenders

Silent and trembling, Aramis rose to his feet. Though able to stand, he was not able to walk. Something of Porthos, now dead, had just died within him. So, the Bretons lifted him gently and carried him to the boat.

Barely half an hour after their sail had been raised, the Bretons spied a white spot on the horizon. But for some time, they did not disturb Aramis, for he seemed lost within himself as if he, too, had departed this world.

An hour passed, and the white spot became a sail. Yves shook Aramis gently.

"Monseigneur, we are being chased!"

Aramis made no reply, and the ship gained upon them. Yves lowered the sail to make their boat more difficult to spot from afar. But that evening, a full moon exposed them to the merciless pursuit of the bigger ship.

A cloud of smoke appeared under the sails. The passengers in the small boat watched as a cannonball bounced across the waves toward them, then sank harmlessly.

"It is a warning to us," said Aramis.

As the night wore on, the vessel drew nearer. At last it came within musketshot. All of its crew were on deck, arms in hand. The cannoneers were at their guns, ready to fire.

"Surrender!" boomed the captain.

The Bretons looked at Aramis for orders. He nodded, and Yves waved a white cloth in the air.

"You shall all go free," announced the captain, "except for Monseigneur d'Herblay."

Aramis paled.

"Shall we accept his terms?" asked Yves.

Yves Waves a White Cloth in the Air.

"Yes," said Aramis, "accept." And he raised his head and drew himself up. With flashing eyes and a smile upon his lips, Aramis addressed the bigger ship as if he, and not its captain, was in command. "Throw out the ladder!"

He was obeyed. Seizing the rope ladder, Aramis ascended the king's ship. Walking up to the captain with a firm step, Aramis surrendered and was led away.

Later that night, Aramis came up on deck and stood looking over the ship's railing in the direction of Belle-Isle. The captain found him there the next morning, in that same spot.

"The night must have been very humid," the captain thought to himself, "for the wooden railing on which the bishop's head had been resting is soaked with dew."

But that dew was, perhaps, the first tears which had ever fallen from the eyes of Aramis d'Herblay—tears of tribute to his good friend Porthos.

Tears of Tribute…

"What Have You to Say to Me?"

CHAPTER 19

D'Artagnan's Decision

Several days later, D'Artagnan arrived at the palace and was shown into the king's rooms. He stood at attention until Louis spoke.

"Well, Monsieur, what have you to say to me?"

"I, Sire?" replied D'Artagnan. "I have nothing to say to Your Majesty. You had me arrested, and here I am."

Louis stared hard at the captain of the musketeers for several moments, then he spoke. "What did I order you to do at Belle-Isle?"

"Why ask me, Sire? Instead, why not ask your officers—those spies who disgraced me before my army?"

"Have you forgotten what your two friends have done to me?" demanded the king. "I lost one hundred six men at Belle-Isle."

D'Artagnan beamed with pride. "And the rebels?" he asked eagerly.

"I truly regret having to tell you that your good friend Porthos lies buried under the rocks of Locmaria."

D'Artagnan paled. "Oh, good Porthos!" he cried. "What a noble life has been sacrificed for the vanity of a king!"

"Monsieur, I am tolerating your words because I understand your grief. However, you may be heartened to know that your friend Aramis has escaped to Spain. But no matter. Let us return to the business that brought you here. Monsieur, you have a choice: Forget what is past, judge me from this day forward, and continue to serve me...

Learning of Porthos' Death!

or…resign and flee into exile!"

"Sire, for thirty years I have served your father in war and you in peace. I have always held a position that permitted me to speak freely to my king. But now it seems that I am simply to be a guard at your doors, groveling at your feet." D'Artagnan sighed, then went on. "If this is so, I shall do it, Sire. Not because I need money, for I have enough. Not because I am ambitious, for I am old and my career will soon come to an end. No, I shall remain because for thirty years my life has been devoted to serving my king."

"Thank you, my faithful friend," said Louis. "Not only will you have my devotion in return, but from this day forward, I shall work toward finding the best opportunity for sending you on a mission in which you can earn the *fleur-de-lis* baton of a marshal—the highest rank an officer can earn."

"Thank you, Sire. That has been my life-long dream."

The Promise of a King's Devotion

Announcing the Arrival of a Visitor

CHAPTER 20

The End of the Musketeers

Four years passed—four years in which D'Artagnan aged twelve. His hair was balding, his face had grown wrinkled, and his beard was white. Still, he sat gracefully and proudly in the saddle.

He had ridden into the forest at Blois this day to join Louis on a hunt, when a messenger approached to announce that the Duke of Almeda had arrived from Spain to visit the king.

"The Duke of Almeda?" said D'Artagnan, puzzling to place the name among the foreign noblemen he knew.

Just then, a carriage pulled up and the door was thrown open.

"It is I!" cried an old man, white as snow, as he came out the door.

"Aramis!" cried D'Artagnan in amazement. And he rushed to embrace his friend warmly.

"I have made peace with Louis," explained Aramis, "and I now serve as the Spanish ambassador to France, bringing Spain's help in his war against Holland."

"A war in which I shall lead Louis' army," said D'Artagnan proudly, "and perhaps, at long last, earn my marshal's baton. In this, I have promised Louis a total victory...or my life!"

"'Tis sad, my friend," said Aramis with a sigh, "that our youth is gone and we cannot fight side by side—the three musketeers who still live."

"Three?...Alas, dear Aramis, then word did not reach you in Spain?...Our dear Athos is dead."

"Aramis!"

"May his soul rest in peace," said Aramis with lowered eyes.

"Do not grieve, dear Aramis. Athos' death was peaceful, I am told. And so, my friend, the four musketeers are now but two."

"Yes, we are now but two," said Aramis, "and I am old and tired. Perhaps when I return to Spain, we may never see each other again."

And the two friends embraced—for what was to be the last time.

That spring, D'Artagnan set out for Holland, the general in command of an army of 12,000 men—men devoted to their skillful, wise and brave leader. After taking twelve cities in a month, D'Artagnan prepared for the final battle of the war.

Upon hearing of these twelve victories, King Louis made ready to keep his promise to D'Artagnan. He placed a small ebony box lined with gold in the hands of an envoy, and

A Last Embrace

sent him, along with a guard of five men, to D'Artagnan's battle site. They arrived on Dutch soil in the midst of a fierce battle that had been going on for five days.

D'Artagnan was standing amid cannon fire on the plain surrounding the besieged city when a voice came up behind him.

"Monsieur D'Artagnan, I have a message from the king. He commands me to inform you that he has named you Marshal of France as a reward for your brilliant services, and he wishes you success in this last siege."

As he finished, the envoy signaled to a guard to bring forward the ebony box. But as the new marshal was accepting it, a loud explosion resounded from the city. D'Artagnan strained to see the city's walls through the smoke.

"It is strange that I do not yet see the French flag flying on the walls," he said. And he ordered an officer to launch one last attack.

Turning his back to the envoy, D'Artagnan raised his hand to open the box. At that

D'Artagnan Is Named Marshal of France.

moment, a cannonball came hurtling toward him, crushing the box in his arms and striking him full in the chest. D'Artagnan fell to the ground in a heap, and the *fleur-de-lis* baton—the long-dreamed-of baton—fell from the box and rolled under his limp hand.

As D'Artagnan struggled to raise himself, a terrible cry broke from his officers. Their beloved leader was covered with blood, and the paleness of death was creeping over his face. Dropping to their knees, the loyal men supported their marshal's head. D'Artagnan turned his eyes toward the city. The white flag of surrender was flying from the walls!

Clutching his marshal's baton in his now numb hand, D'Artagnan cast his closing eyes down on it, murmuring, "Athos, Porthos, *au revoir!* Aramis, *adieu* forever...."

Of the four brave men who changed the course of the history of France, there remained but one. The days of the musketeers had drawn to a close.

"*Au Revoir* and *Adieu* Forever...."